D1250067

Winning Scheherazade

Winning Scheherazade

Judith Gorog

atheneum 1991 new york
Collier Macmillan Canada
TORONTO
Maxwell Macmillan International Publishing Group
NEW YORK OXFORD SINGAPORE SYDNEY

Atheneum
Macmillan Publishing Company
866 Third Avenue
New York, NY 10022

Collier Macmillan Canada, Inc.
1200 Eglinton Avenue East
Suite 200
Don Mills, Ontario M3C 3N1

First edition
Printed in the United States of America
1 2 3 4 5 6 7 8 9 10
Designed by Kimberly M. Hauck

Library of Congress Cataloging-in-Publication Data
Gorog, Judith.
Winning Scheherazade/Judith Gorog.
p. cm.
Summary: Having been released from her position as storyteller and doomed bride of the sultan, Scheherazade is propelled by a mysterious visitor into dangerous adventures in the desert.
ISBN 0–689–31648–8
1. Scheherazade (Legendary character)—Juvenile fiction.
[1. Scheherazade (Legendary character)—Fiction. 2. Adventure and adventurers—Fiction.] I. Title.
PZ7.G673Wi 1991
[Fic]—dc20

For Pamela McCorduck,
who loves to hear a good story,
lives a good story,
and writes a good story

Author's Note

The retelling of Scheherazade that begins this book came about one day several years ago when I was talking with a group of students who said they did not know the story of Scheherazade. I told it then as I remembered it, from a reading perhaps ten or even fifteen years earlier. When I later reread a version of the story of the Arabian nights in my local library, I was surprised to notice how greatly I had changed the story from the version I found in that book. Out of that difference, in part, grew this book. The mysterious visitor tells his version of the story; again his telling comes out of his character telling the story as I remember it from my more recent reading. Of the tales that follow, all but two are ones I have "made up," as we used to call the process when I was a child. Of the old stories, the one about the "magic white pebbles" (which are, of course, garlic) is clearly a retelling of *Stone Soup.* The Sultan tells an old Indian tale, that of the golden parrot, in his own version, again as I remember it from wherever I read it years ago.

The desire to write of Scheherazade arose in part out of a book I have enjoyed, recommended countless times, and continue to recommend. Inea Bushnaq's skill takes those of us who are outsiders into the family circle, where we can sit, unremarked, and listen to stories of wit, courage, and boundless generosity: *Arab Folktales,* translated and edited by Inea Bushnaq, Pantheon Fairy Tale and Folklore Library, New York, 1988.

Winning Scheherazade

Prologue

There once lived a Sultan who had absolute power of life and death over every creature within his realm. It was that Sultan's pleasure that the most beautiful, most accomplished young women in the land should be brought, one by one, with the long shadows of each afternoon, brought one each day to him to be his bride. And every morning, after the sun had risen, the Sultan had the young woman killed.

Needless to say, there was not a girl in all that kingdom who desired to be the Sultan's bride. Nevertheless, night after night, the brides appeared, for the Sultan had made it a crime to hide a girl, to attempt to bribe an official charged with obtaining the girls, or to maim a girl so that she should be less than perfect. In short, to make any attempt to save a child or a sister or a cousin was to be slain and to have the girl and all the family slain, and to have whatever the family possessed taken into the Sultan's coffers.

And so it was that Scheherazade, who had been raised by the Bedouins of the desert sands on the very edge of the Sultan's kingdom, was nevertheless discovered and brought to the palace, unprotesting, to be the Sultan's bride.

Her parents, who were dwelling in a town at the edge of the desert, turned their eyes from the bride price left by the Sultan's officials. Her brothers, however, picked up the bags of gold and set off to give the money to the poor, so that every last coin should be gone before their sister was slain.

Scheherazade made no resistance while the women of the harem silently bathed and dressed her, perfumed the palms of her hands and the soles of her feet, and put upon her arms and neck precious jewels.

Girls had tried to win the Sultan, tried with music, with dancing, even with loving charms, in every possible way, or so everyone thought. All had failed.

At last, as the long shadows fell across the room, Scheherazade was alone with the Sultan. Calmly she sat herself upon a cushion and began to speak. "There once was, so the old ones say, a king . . ."

The Sultan leaned forward to catch her low tones, forgetting everything else as that first tale, which held within it yet another story, beguiled its way into another and into still another so that dawn broke upon a story still unfinished. And the Sultan ordered that Scheherazade should live for one more night.

When evening came, Scheherazade began where she had left off. Then, never missing a beat, she went from that tale into the telling of a tale so terrifying that in his heart the Sultan longed to look behind him to be certain it was not true, but not once did he take his eyes from Scheherazade as she spoke. Again the sun rose upon a tale unfinished, and again the Sultan ordered that Scheherazade should live.

After seven nights, when Scheherazade was once again brought alive and well to them in their quarters, the women of the harem dared to befriend her, making certain she had a quiet place in which to sleep away a portion of the day, bringing her fruits and honeyed drinks to keep her voice well and strong. They made music for her, asked no questions of her, and tried not to show their fear for her as the seven days and nights became seventeen, and then seventy.

And every day Scheherazade's parents and brothers dreaded the arrival of the message that would order them to the palace to fetch her body for burial. And still the messenger did not come, and slowly they dared to hope that perhaps Scheherazade would give the Sultan a child and then he would surely spare her, but the days became weeks and months and still they could not see her, and heard only that she lived, lived and there was no child, only the stories that followed one after another, night after night.

As they had vowed, Scheherazade's brothers went out every night to distribute alms among the poor. That first night, they had given away the gold of the bride price. When it was gone, they gave their own, and as the pile of coins dwindled, other coins came to them in mysterious bundles. For it was true that the families of other girls in the Sultan's kingdom looked at one another and said, "So long as Scheherazade lives, the Sultan does not take our daughters, sisters, and intended brides. We must help her brothers in their vow."

And Scheherazade? At first, her spirits soared with relief as yet another dawn appeared in the window of the Sultan's chamber. But as the days became weeks and then months and a year, a year of days spent locked in the Sultan's palace, with only a slice of sky visible between the tops of the high palace walls and the roofs that shaded palace and garden from the blazing sun, the girl languished. Thoughts of home pushed unbidden into her days, whether she slept or woke. Now, she thought, now the white mare my father gave me has surely foaled. And the young colt that is the son of the same swift parents, surely he is already a stallion. And the weaving begun last year is surely complete . . . and my little black goat . . . To stop herself, Scheherazade danced, even in the heat of midday when all the harem slept.

Sometimes the others awoke, rose from their couches, urged her to stop. Sometimes they laughed to see her imitate in dance the gait of her father's camels. Sometimes they sighed in amazement when she whirled, with bells on her ankles and tiny cymbals on her slender fingers, dancing in furious, wild, sad rhythms until she collapsed with exhaustion. The others nursed her, coaxed her to eat, prepared her, and sent her off each evening to sit before the Sultan for what might be the very last time.

And each time Scheherazade returned with the dawn, the others in the harem rejoiced.

And so it was that Scheherazade told the Sultan stories for one thousand nights and one night.

And as that last dawn filled the sky, Scheherazade came to the end of her story, a story so impossibly funny that tears of laughter flooded the Sultan's eyes and coursed freely down his cheeks. Scheherazade said,

"We left them happy, and back we came.
May Allah make your life the same."

To which the Sultan, wiping the tears from his eyes and bowing his head, replied, "Praise be to Allah!"

In the silence that followed, Scheherazade, bowing low before she spoke, slowly said, "Sire, I have finished my tales."

"Finished?" replied the Sultan, at once serious and disbelieving. "No more?"

"I have finished," she repeated. "It is too painful for my family to wait every morning for news of my death, too painful for me to live a prisoner in your palace."

"Princess," the Sultan replied. "You are too harsh. I am not the only threat to your parents' joy, nor are you more a prisoner here than any modest maiden would be in her father's house. If I have gained nothing else from your stories, I have learned that news of our death may stun our loved ones at any moment."

"True."

"But," continued the Sultan, "you have been generous with your tales. Demand anything, unto half my kingdom. It is yours."

Scheherazade bowed low, straightened herself, and replied, "I wish only my freedom, Sire."

"That, too, you shall have, and a palace, and from this day you are the Princess Scheherazade, Storyteller of Our Kingdom, free to come and go between the sands and tents of the far desert and your palace, beyond, even into the most distant corners of our kingdom."

"And your brides?" asked Scheherazade.

The Sultan looked down at his hands. "They shall live. I have done with all that. I swear it to you."

Scheherazade bowed once again.

Rising from the cushion on which he had sat, the Sultan walked toward her and gave her his hands so that she, too, should stand. "Go now, Princess, and God go with you." He paused a moment, then released her hands. Leaning toward her, he whispered, "I do, dear Princess"—he dropped his voice still lower—"do trust that I have permission to hear a story now and again."

And Scheherazade, who was as wise in the ways of the powerful as she was beautiful to the eye, replied, "Of course."

Chapter One

In the time before time, when all these many things took place, the Princess Scheherazade, honored teller of many tales, lived in a modest palace with some of her brothers and sisters and their wives, husbands, and children in a town at the edge of the vast desert. There she was served by those who came to learn from her the legends, songs, and poems from times long past and lands near and far.

It was said throughout the land that Scheherazade was wise and kind and more beautiful than a full moon of the night. In the morning of the first day after the month-long fast of Ramadan, a stranger stood in the throng at the gates of Scheherazade's palace. As was the custom and duty of every child of Allah, Scheherazade and her family gave food to the poor at the end of every day during the fast of Ramadan and provided a feast for the poor after the fast had ended.

The stranger quietly waited until he reached the gate. When greeted by the servants, the stranger replied most courteously and from his cloak drew forth a small package wrapped in silk of midnight blue, tied with threads of silver. This he gave to one of the servants, saying that by the grace of Allah he had journeyed from afar to bring this small gift for the Princess.

After asking the stranger to wait within the gate of the courtyard, the girl raced through the rooms to where Scheherazade sat reading. "A stranger," reported the breathless girl, "wearing garments worn with travel, but of fine quality, a stranger with a voice to make the heart beat faster . . . and eyes, dark and sad . . . sends this gift and awaits in the court beside the gate."

The girl stood watching while Scheherazade unwrapped the silk to discover a box the size of the palm of her hand. It was made of silver filigree, lined with silk of midnight blue. On the silk lay a small silver elephant. "Ooh," sighed the girl.

Scheherazade picked up the silver figure, stood it on the palm of her hand. She marveled at this most curious elephant, with its head down, trunk down, and most curious of all, a diamond on its cheek, a diamond that looked for all the world like a tear falling from the baby elephant's eye.

Scheherazade asked that the visitor be welcomed and all the honors of a guest accorded him. Then, for the two days during which tradition requires that a guest receive every courtesy and care before any questions may be asked of him, the servants attended the stranger, and the family made him welcome. One after another, the women of the household, young and old, sighed at his grave good looks, at his bearing, at his voice, his eyes.

In the afternoon of the second day, Scheherazade greeted her guest as he walked in the garden. "May Allah give you long life and good health."

"Grateful, indeed, am I for His blessings, and for the hospitality of your house," replied the guest.

Then, for the second time, Scheherazade offered him the place of honor at the evening meal.

The visitor sat down, accepted food and drink. The mysterious guest then began to praise most eloquently and at great length the beauties of the garden, the architecture of the house, the music played softly in the background. These praises he had already most fulsomely made during the hours of feasting on the previous day. Scheherazade replied, as she had on the previous day, courteously, wondering all the while what it was that brought this visitor to her gates. He looked young, but too wellborn to have come to learn to be a teller of tales.

The stranger talked on, drawing out the gently flattering small talk of the visitor to an interminable length. Surely he was no suitor. Suitors never arrived as worn and dusty travelers, grateful for the courtesy extended to all who requested it. Why then had he come? And for what reason had he chosen to give a silver elephant with a tear on its cheek?

Every member of the household was there at the evening meal, each drawn to the handsome stranger with the beautiful voice. And still he talked on, quoting from the great poets of the past, and from the songs sung that day in the marketplace, all in praise of the garden, the palace, the desert nearby. Certainly, Scheherazade thought to herself, he was learned, but why so long-winded?

The evening of that second day led into the night, and lamps were brought to light the rooms. And then that entertainment, too, drew to a close without any of them knowing more of the visitor's purpose. When they met on the third day, the compliments continued; furthermore, the visitor showed no sign that he intended to adhere to custom, which would demand that he not linger past dawn of the fourth morning. Once again the household feasted in honor of the mysterious guest.

By this time, Scheherazade was quite actively longing for the visitor to depart, even if he never gave reason for his visit. While feigning attention, she began to plot how she would send for all the rest of her family, and for many other guests to draw this one away into conversation so that she could escape him.

Thus occupied with her thoughts, Scheherazade abruptly became aware that the visitor was silent, that no one in all the room was making the slightest sound. Scheherazade looked up from the flower she had been pretending to study. The stranger, his large, dark eyes full of sadness, stared openly at her. Startled, Scheherazade asked, "Are you ill, honored guest?"

"No, not ill in the usual sense," responded the visitor. "My pain springs from another source, from cruel injustice."

"How can that be?" replied Scheherazade.

There was once a Sultan, replied the guest, shaking his head slowly in a great show of sorrow. Happiest of men, he was married to a wife of beauty and grace. Dwelling in perfect bliss, grateful to Allah for all his blessings, he bade his greatly treasured wife farewell and traveled away from home one day to visit his brother, who was Sultan in another city. Our Sultan was scarcely an hour away from the white walls of his own palace when he discovered that he had forgotten to bring with him a jeweled sword, a gift for his brother.

As his was the fleetest and freshest horse of all in his company, he decided to return to his home for the sword. No sooner had he rushed, unannounced, into his palace, than he discovered his treasure, his wife, in the arms of a foul and greasy cook, the chief roaster of meats from his kitchen!

Though his eyes were full of tears, the Sultan dispatched them both with one blow of his sword.

Heartbroken at his wife's betrayal, he took up the gift sword for his brother, stumbled from his palace, mounted his horse, and galloped back to his company. Without a word to his companions, he continued on his journey, reaching his brother's palace two days later. There he gave himself up fully to his sorrow, eating nothing, sleeping not at all, suffering night and day at the cruelty of his faithless wife. Though his brother tried hard to comfort him, it was of no avail. After some days, his brother said, "Come. Let us take our hawks and go to hunt. It is not good for man nor beast to mourn so. Your hawks, your horses, all your servants suffer with you. Rise up, now!" But the Sultan refused, saying that the others should go without him, which they did.

The hunting party had been gone but half an hour when the Sultan rose from his bed, thinking that his brother had told truth and that he should bestir himself to life again. Going forth out of his room, what should he see but his brother's beloved wife! She, the fair, much-honored one, raced the length of the garden, ran straight into the arms of a monstrous, greasy cook who stood grinning, open armed, reeking of the fats of roasting meats!

Taking up his sword, the twice brokenhearted Sultan killed the lustful betrayers with one blow. Blind with sorrow, he left his brother's palace. Taking his horse from the stables, he rode swiftly after the hunting party.

Imagine his brother's joyful surprise to see our Sultan striding toward him. Then, imagine our Sultan's subdued and loving greeting. Imagine how he whispers to his brother that they must walk a little apart from the others.

Upon hearing of his much-loved wife's loathsome faithlessness, the Sultan's brother gave one single brokenhearted cry and fell to the ground, dead.

With this new grief heavy upon him, our Sultan returned to his city, vowing never again to be betrayed by woman. To this end, he took a new wife every night. Each and every new wife was put to death the following morning. Never, ever again would our Sultan suffer from the faithlessness of women.

In time, news of the Sultan's stern command had a sobering effect upon the girls and women of the kingdom.

In time, the daughter of the Sultan's vizir grew to be a graceful maiden. In time, that maiden went to her father and demanded that she become the Sultan's bride. The vizir protested. No. Never so long as he should be the Sultan's trusted adviser. She, she alone of all the maidens in the kingdom was safe from the Sultan's just anger. Nevertheless, the vizir's daughter persisted. She *would be* the Sultan's bride. Sadly, the vizir told the Sultan of his daughter's wish. Sternly, the Sultan warned his vizir that the girl must suffer the same fate as the others. There could be no trust granted to any of womankind. The vizir bowed his acknowledgment and sadly returned home.

With this, the girl became the Sultan's bride and did spend tender hours with him. After they had slept for some time, she offered the Sultan, her husband, food and drink, which she had asked her sister to bring to them. The Sultan took of the food and drink, thanking the sister, who bowed low to the Sultan, then turned to her sister, the bride, and said, "Ahh, Scheherazade," for that was the young bride's name, "can you tell us a story to while away the remaining hours of the night?"

With this, said the visitor, Scheherazade began the tale of the faithless wife of the Djinn who owned the wind mare and the rain mare.

* * *

As the visitor told his tale of Scheherazade and related the tales she told, all the servants stopped still where they stood to listen to the telling.

The Princess listened carefully, although she knew every single one of the stories at least as well as her visitor. She listened and wondered, where *was* the stranger leading them? Skillfully, he hooked the tendril of one story into another until the Princess called for the lamps to be brought, until she called for coffee to be served, until she longed to yawn, longed for the stranger to go to his evening rest. Still he told on, one story after another, some to make the listener laugh, some to make one weep, but all of them, each and every one, stories about the perfidy of women.

"Ahh. His eyes," sighed the maid who took the jewels from Scheherazade's hands. "Ahh," she sighed again, gazing at the ropes of pearls as she put them into their casket. "Did you see the sadness in his eyes?"

"I did," sighed the second maid, tenderly embracing a satin cushion. "How I long to console him."

"You could rub his feet," suggested the first maid, giggling.

"With pleasure." The second smiled.

"If you have need of conversation"—Scheherazade's voice betrayed only the smallest trace of the irritation she felt—"then please take yourselves elsewhere. I am very sleepy."

"But, Princess"—the girls giggled—"what do you say of our guest, and of the tales he tells?"

"They show," replied Scheherazade as she lay down, closing her weary eyes, "a certain lack of variety." With that, she appeared to be asleep.

Still whispering, the maids went to their sleeping places, where they dreamed away what remained of the night.

Many hours later, the rays of the morning sun reached, then warmed her face, but Scheherazade turned away. She would not awaken.

What could she do to escape her guest? Should she have ridden into the desert before dawn? Should she feign illness and imprison herself in her rooms? And for how long? Last night he had shown no sign that he ever intended to leave. There were, Scheherazade knew, many, many more stories about the unfaithfulness of women. Humph, and an equal number about faithless men . . . and cruel men, stupid men, and, she had to admit, stupid women and greedy men and women . . . Such thoughts led nowhere. She sighed. How to avoid the guest?

Auntie Berthe appeared, ignoring Scheherazade's pretended sleep. "Here now, my dear flower, this tea of mint and honey will give you strength for the day ahead . . . and your bath all ready . . . and you lying abed. . . ." Her voice trailed off for a moment, but almost immediately she reappeared, clearly prepared to lift the girl from her bed and carry her to the bath should there be any further resistance.

"I am up. Thank you," grumbled Scheherazade, taking the tea and drinking it thirstily.

"He *does* have a beautiful voice," remarked Auntie Berthe, as if they were continuing a conversation begun earlier. "And the muscles rippled under his skin—ahh, that smooth skin—with the color and texture of—"

"You, too, are under his spell!" Scheherazade laughed, pretending a careless amusement at this constant praise of the stranger. "Auntie, Auntie, shame on you. After all of life that you have seen."

"Mmm," replied Auntie, looking critically at the girl. "Mmm."

Scheherazade, refusing to ask the reason for the look, or for the murmuring, went to her bath. When she returned to her room, the Princess Storyteller took longer than ever she had in her life to find garments to wear. Not that she wanted to impress the guest, not at all. She tried only to draw out the day in order to make shorter the time she would be forced to endure his tales, tales that all the others in the household seemed to enjoy so much.

Listening to him was unbearable. She knew that every tale was told as a reproach to her, a denial of her own thousand and one nights of tales. And what reason had he for those suggestions that he, like the Sultan of his story, had suffered at the hands of a cruel woman?

Bah! Let the others comfort him. All of them. She would not.

As these thoughts trampled through her mind, Scheherazade tried and tossed garment after garment, knowing that the maids whispered and giggled. Naturally, they, in their simplicity, assumed that she, too, had been smitten by the charms of the visitor. It was not true!

Bah!

At last, she could compose herself, could prepare to walk down to the garden, where her guest would surely be waiting. Her guest. Ha. Her tormentor. No. No such thoughts. She must be calm. Perhaps she should suggest that they take a ride into the desert this evening. At least, on horseback he could not talk all the time. The moon would be . . . Ah. Let them think her smitten.

She longed to ride in the desert. The more she thought of it, the better the idea seemed . . . unless she could have her family entertain the guest, and she escape alone to ride. That idea was the most attractive but seemed impossible. Her rudeness to the guest would be remarked, her family shamed. No. She should invite him. But, then, his very rudeness in remaining past the three and one-third days that tradition accorded . . . and . . . As she walked and debated with herself, Scheherazade failed to notice the commotion that buzzed around her, all the servants chattering, sisters, brothers, children, and adults running to and fro.

Thus unaware, she went into the garden, walked beneath the trees, all the way to the far wall, to a bench near the smallest fountain, where she could sit in quiet. And there she was alone. And there she could think and sit in solitude, in complete solitude, until slowly she became aware that she was very hungry. And further became aware that she had been a very long time in the garden by the small fountain. All that time no one had come to look for her, and she was truly surprised. And after more time passed, and still no one came to look for her, Scheherazade got up from her bench and walked back into the palace. There she saw the most amazing sight.

Maids, cooks, serving boys and girls, her aunts, uncles, and cousins, her brothers and sisters and their wives and husbands, all of the ones who had come to learn the telling of stories, and those who taught the children their lessons—in short, every living being in her palace could be seen together in the main courtyard if not leaning and calling from balconies as if in a great market. Some were sitting surrounded by silks. Some ran excitedly back and forth to look and admire and to show and beam at the praise received. Not one of them took notice of Scheherazade standing there gazing at them in stunned bewilderment. Slowly, Scheherazade was able to separate the buzz of their chatter into words and phrases: so good . . . so generous . . . so sad . . . some secret sorrow. . . .

All at once, they noticed her and hastened to tell her the news, everyone speaking at once in a rising crescendo so that poor Scheherazade was forced to cover her ears with her hands until they were silent. With a gesture, her eldest brother sent the entire household back to its normal routine, and then took Scheherazade by the arm and led her back into the garden.

"Ahh, little one," he began.

Scheherazade shuddered. There was that *ahh* again. Surely all of this had something to do with the visitor who had so besotted every member of her household.

"Here, let us sit for a moment. You are pale, little star. I'll send for some food."

"No. Please, first tell me," asked Scheherazade.

"Of course. Did you know that our guest was called away suddenly before dawn?"

"No." She'd not have wasted the morning had she

known. What did his departure mean? What an annoying man he was.

"Shortly after his departure," her eldest brother began, "he had sent word that you were not to be disturbed, and had sent his profound regrets and apologies for the rudeness of his leavetaking."

"Yes. Yes. Yes." Must she bear the stranger's longwindedness even when he was finally, blessedly, gone?

"Shortly after his departure . . . but did you know the . . . curious question he asked everyone . . . everyone in the household? Did he ask you, little sister?"

"Ask me?"

"He asked us . . . so many of us . . . if we knew the story . . . of . . . the Reluctant Betrothéd Pair. I don't know it. Do you?"

"Never mind his stories. You were telling me about his departure."

"Curious . . . yes . . . as I was saying, shortly after his departure, a caravan bearing gifts for the entire household arrived, each gift especially selected to give unbounded joy to the recipient. How well he knows your family and household, little sister! Again, messages accompanied each gift, and a declaration that he owes to you his life and his future. . . . Who is he that he is so knowing of us and so devoted?"

"His servants gave no name?"

"Only names of praise and honor." Eldest Brother

chuckled. "He also offered, before he left, encouragement and certain gentle suggestions to cook about the seasoning of one or two dishes, and to the head gardener about—"

"Suggestions they certainly plan most graciously to ignore," growled Scheherazade. More than ever, she needed to ride free in the desert. This meddling visitor had thoroughly disturbed the tranquillity of her household and now from afar continued to jerk the strings he had tied to her family and servants as if they were so many little puppets!

Ah! She forced herself to breathe slowly. She should not blaze this way. Surely if she could remain calm, the excitement of his visit and gifts would last a few days at best. She'd ride out to the tents of her great-uncle, to the desert place. There this petty annoyance would fall away from her.

Having made her decision, Scheherazade spent the remainder of the day quietly preparing to leave for the desert. In normal times, she'd simply have taken her horse and gone out the gate, but today she had to restore what measure she could of order and tranquillity to her household. All the rest of the day she gently, quietly directed them so that they should not be too greatly swayed by the dark eyes and bright gifts of the mysterious visitor. To this end, she had to admire every gift, to praise it and the recipient and then to suggest a program to be followed during her absence. She also had to promise that all who desired to go with her to the desert could accompany her *soon,* surely before the next full moon. For now, she needed solitude.

The cool, long shadows of evening stretched across the stable courtyard when Scheherazade led out her mare, saddled and dancing with the excitement that filled them both. One soft boot in the stirrup, one small pull up into the saddle, and—

And before she could mount, Scheherazade saw the gate swing open to admit a beaming messenger leading behind him an excited group of children, beggars, servants, and passersby, all surrounding the "Gift for the Princess! Gift for the Princess!" he so joyfully announced. "An incomparable gift for an incomparable Princess," and many more words to that effect.

Thanking him, asking the servants to offer him refreshments, sending the crowd to be fed, handing her drooping mare to be led away by a groom, Scheherazade approached the gift. Poor little thing. Who would be so cruel as to separate it from its own kind? What kind of madman would ever dream that she would welcome such a present?

In the empty courtyard, Scheherazade slowly, with her hand outstretched, approached the elephant baby. The baby put its trunk into her palm, snuffling softly. Could it even eat without its mother? Stroking first its side, and then its broad head, and she sighed. "If you are alive," she told it, "then your mother cannot be so very far away. We'll find her, but first see if you can drink water."

Leading the baby to the fountain, Scheherazade put her hand into the water. The baby followed with its trunk but did not drink. "Are you not thirsty?" The Princess sighed. "Or are you too sad to drink?"

chapter Two

By *moonrise, certain members of the household* had reason to suspect that perhaps the Princess Scheherazade was less than enchanted with their mysterious guest and the gift he had sent her. Servants had been sent running from the palace with orders not to return until they brought with them the mother of the elephant baby. It had also been made clear to them that the orphaned baby must have its mother soon. No! *Immediately!* Upon their departure, the rest of the household was ordered to bed. The silent palace stood pale in the moonlight.

To the baby elephant, Scheherazade offered a goatskin bottle she had filled with milk and honey. No matter how she coaxed, the baby refused. From her cupped hands, he did take a few drops, not nearly enough to sustain him.

In her stall, the mare whickered piteously, so that Scheherazade brought her out to join the elephant in the courtyard, where the three of them waited away the night. The girl covered the mare, the elephant, and herself with horse quilts. All the while she murmured promises to the elephant that his mother would soon be there, promises she hoped were true.

Morning came and went. Scheherazade petted and coaxed the baby, then groomed her mare to soothe the jealousy excited by the attentions she had lavished upon the elephant.

Shortly after afternoon prayers, a tremendous commotion arose outside the palace gates. The hooves of horses clattering on the cobblestones mingled with the thump of running feet and with pleas cried out to heaven for mercy. Ultimately, all other sounds were drowned out by the trumpeting of an angry elephant. The gates crashed open before a tumbling, shouting throng. Trunk held high, the baby elephant raced toward his mother. The crowd did well to part before him, for there was the look of blood in the mother elephant's eye, a look that promised death to anyone or anything that stood between her and her found one.

Scheherazade had time neither to rejoice that the

orphan had been reunited with his mother nor to give herself up to the fury she felt toward her visitor and his ill-considered gifts, because she was immediately accosted by seven officers of the royal police, a black-bearded giant who bellowed that he was the owner of the elephants, various onlookers who offered themselves as witnesses, and her own bedraggled servants, who stood before her weeping—and in chains.

A full two days and nights later, the Princess Scheherazade, her eyes two dark circles of fatigue, crawled onto her waiting bed. Once more her household was at peace, and at what a price. The police had arrested her servants for attempting to steal the mother elephant, whose owner accused them of having stolen the baby in the first place. Of course, his story could not be true. Who on earth could take a baby elephant from its living mother? But how, then, had the baby been taken? And why, why would it seem a gift to give? Those questions, and a good many more, went unanswered, although there had been talk and argument enough to fill ten thousand days and nights, had not all those concerned spent a great deal of time shouting at and above one another. It gave Scheherazade a headache to remember it. Had she not made liberal use of *baksheesh* and soft words, the whole crowd would be arguing still. She sighed.

The gate was repaired, the servants and elephants restored to their places, the police praised and rewarded for their vigilance, the elephant owner consoled with lavish gifts, and a tear dried from the cheek of the baby elephant. Now, at last, she could sleep and dream that tomorrow, indeed, she would escape with her mare to the desert.

The stars had begun to fade from the sky when, somewhere in the palace, someone began to play softly upon a flute. The song made its way into more than one dream that morning, gently weaving in and out of the images that moved behind eyes that slept. The song that someone played in the darkness had its cheerful moments but ended on a note of such longing that more than one person awoke hours later to find the pillow wet from weeping.

One person was awakened by the song, listened, and did not sleep again. After a time, Scheherazade crept from her couch, washed her face, and said her prayers. So silently that the others never stirred in their sleep, she took out her clothes: cotton pantaloons for riding, her cloak and boots. Quickly she dressed, braided her hair, then stole down to the pantry, where she filled a leather pouch with bread, dates, and goat cheese.

Leaving the kitchen, Scheherazade ran across the stable courtyard, made her way swiftly into the stable.

In minutes, the first of the stable boys and grooms would be awake and about. As the Princess approached, the mare shifted impatiently in her stall but made no sound. Giving her a carrot and a whispered greeting, Scheherazade bridled and saddled the mare, then led her from the stable. Taking the mare through the small side gate, Scheherazade reached the street. There she mounted and rode out of the town and into the desert as the first light of dawn lined the horizon with silver.

In the cool of the early morning, Scheherazade rode to an oasis not far from the city, where she hoped to find news of her great-uncle, the brother of her grandfather. To his tents, she would make her way after the heat of midday had passed. Indeed, at that oasis she met with herders who told her where her great-uncle's flocks were pastured, where his tents were to be found, and then invited her to visit with them and rest with them. She accepted coffee and honey cakes. She heard news and gossip of that place and was not in the least surprised to learn that the story of her elephant baby had already been told and retold at that oasis. She sighed. No doubt the story would travel both faster and farther than she herself.

Through the evening, Scheherazade rode without reaching the place where she had been told she'd find her great-uncle. No matter—the mare was fresh, and the moon soon would rise to light the way. Scheherazade, feeling her heart grow lighter with each step the mare took, rode on into the desert.

But as quickly as news travels in the desert, the tents of the Bedouins are often moved more quickly. Scheherazade had sent no message ahead to her great-uncle that she traveled to meet with him. And so it was that no child had been set to watch for her approach. No scent of coffee filled the air. When she reached the place where she expected to meet her great-uncle, she found water and trees and signs that humans and animals had recently dwelt there, but not a tent was to be seen. Having grazed their flocks for as long as the fodder would bear, her great-uncle and all his clan had broken camp and moved on.

Scheherazade dismounted. Both she and the mare needed to sleep. Tomorrow they would surely reach Great-uncle's new resting place. For now, they had food and water and were at peace with the night and the desert.

The stars were still bright when Scheherazade awoke. She washed her face and said her prayers, braided her hair, then groomed and saddled the mare. The trail her great-uncle had taken was clear, a simple matter to follow even by starlight. Scheherazade sat easily in the saddle, permitting her mind to wander, to amble and meander over and around the events of the past days without any attempt to make sense of what had happened. There would be time, later. Now only the mare's hoof falls in the sand and the rhythmic creak of the saddle could be heard in the still space.

Scheherazade closed her eyes, the better to feel every breath. Slowly filling her lungs, she held the night air inside her for a few seconds before slowly releasing it. The taste of the city was gone from her mouth. In time, her head would clear. Everything connected with the visitor was behind her. She laughed aloud. Not quite everything, for the story would reach her great-uncle long before she did. And then, and then . . . Scheherazade sighed. True, true. She would find her great-uncle and greet him and all the family. By the time they had drunk two cups of coffee, her uncles and aunts would turn the talk to marriage. Ah, yes. Marriage.

Back then, on the first day after she had returned home from the Sultan's palace, free—free and called the Princess Storyteller—Scheherazade had bowed low to thank her brothers for their thousand and one nights of almsgiving and prayers for her safety. Her family had rejoiced at her return. All had rejoiced that the Sultan would no longer kill his wives. Then, after the first joy of reunion had passed, her family had asked her whether the Sultan had forbidden her to marry. No. "Well, then," her whole great family had sighed with joy. "We must find you a husband." Scheherazade had asked for time.

Now three full years had passed. Suitors had come unbidden. She had rejected them all. The whole great family whispered of growing disappointment with her.

She knew that when she arrived at the tents of her great-uncle, her aunts would cluck over her. They would show her babies, new cousins, born since her last visit. When she held the babies, she would feel that, indeed, she wanted one of her own.

But. But. Marriage. Her aunts and cousins would urge her to hurry . . . hurry before she became old and unmarriageable.

What manner of husband did she want? If he did her bidding, the family would laugh at him. If she did his, they'd laugh at her and say that finally she'd been brought down from her high horse. Ahh. Shaking such thoughts away, she told herself to concentrate only on the smells of the night. Was there water nearby? Or the scent of a night-blooming plant?

Under her knees, the mare tensed. Scheherazade opened her eyes. The mare's ears twitched nervously back and forth. Her pace faltered as she turned her head. Scheherazade looked in the same direction. From over the rise came a rider, an ancient patriarch, to judge by the brilliant white of his beard and hair. He rode a fine old stallion, which pranced and flared its nostrils as he came alongside the mare.

"May Allah go with you, Granddaughter," the old gentleman greeted her.

"And with you, Grandfather," the girl replied, bowing to his years. By his robes, he must be a great sheikh, though he rode unattended at night. Perhaps he, too, went into the desert when sleep deserted him.

"Ah," said the old man. "You are following the trail of my kinsman."

"Yes. He is my great-uncle, sir."

"His tents are far from here, not to be reached until another day has passed. Before you travel farther, you should come to rest and share the meals of our family. My dear wife, my daughters, and granddaughters—all will have great joy in your company, child. You and I will hear the welcome sound of many women beating coffee beans long before we reach the tents, so great will be my wife's joy at a granddaughter visitor."

"Thank you, Grandfather. It would be an honor, but cruel of me to cut short the sleep of your family."

"No, no, no," insisted the old gentleman, his shaggy white eyebrows moving rapidly up and down as he spoke. "It is very nearly dawn. All the people of my household will be awake and about. Time for food and guests."

With that, Scheherazade bowed and turned the mare to follow the old man.

Indeed, his tents were not far, and at their arrival a servant sprang forth to take the horses with words of praise for the beauty and grace of the mare.

At the opening of the largest of the tents, the smell of fresh coffee did fill the air. A servant whispered that the mistress awaited inside. The old man strode in, saying, "And while we eat, we'll ask of my auntie that she tell us a story, a favorite of mine, that of the Reluctant Bethrothéd Pair. Do you know it?"

Scheherazade, following close behind the old man, started. That story? "Once I have heard it named, but never heard the tale," she replied.

Scheherazade looked around, expecting to see an old lady, wife to the sheikh, and perhaps daughters and servants. The tent, most luxuriously appointed, was empty. She turned to question her host, but the old man suddenly clutched at his chest with a loud groan. Scheherazade ran to his side.

Falling to the carpet at her feet, he cried out, "Ahhh! The pain! I am dead!" After two convulsive kicks, he was still.

At this, from every side, men rushed into the tent, shouting, "Harlot! You have killed our master! Thief! Murderer!"

"No," cried the Princess. "No. Quickly, we must do something for him. He is ill."

The servants hurled themselves at her, striking at her, some of them attempting to grab hold of her.

Scheherazade stepped backward to avoid their blows. As she did so, all light abruptly disappeared. Scheherazade was thrown to the ground under the weight of the tent that collapsed upon them.

In the scramble of people snarled among the hangings, skins, and carpets that had once been a tent, Scheherazade choked on the dust that filled her eyes and mouth. She managed to pull herself into a crouch, tried to think how to crawl out. There was a great deal of shouting, wailing, "Our Master is slain. Capture her. Kill the harlot!" Beneath the folds of cloth, someone took hold of her arm, whispered, tried to lead Scheherazade from the melee. "Come," the voice whispered again. "They will kill you. Follow me, and we'll be safe."

Crawling out from beneath the tent, her eyes still filled with dust, Scheherazade followed the dark shadow ahead of her. Abruptly, the figure rose to a crouch, reached back, grabbed her hand, led her at a run over a dune to a place apart from the tents. There some horses were tethered. "Here. Mount, ride, follow me." Her rescuer, a dirty, ragged fellow, leaped into the saddle of an aged nag. Scheherazade followed, onto the back of an equally miserable-looking horse. When had a great sheikh ever had such animals, even for pack horses? No matter, they had to ride, and quickly, before the others would find she was not trapped under the tent.

"Who are you? What happened there?" she gasped, as they urged the horses to a faster pace.

"A prisoner, forced into slavery, captured in a raid. Don't worry. I know of a place close enough that even these horses can make the journey. We'll be safe there. In such a place, these are the sort of horses anyone would expect to find." He spat out the words in scorn.

Her companion rode with great skill, so that even the miserable beasts on which they rode moved like true horses, soon leaving the tents of the old sheikh far behind.

After a time, he signaled to slow the pace. They rode in silence while the horses rested. Then, without urging, their mounts pricked their ears, picked up their pace, and went as if they knew the road, straight to a wretched collection of mud huts. And there the panting beasts stopped.

Not a soul emerged to greet them. Scheherazade's companion dismounted. Scheherazade followed suit. He led his mount into a ramshackle shed attached to the back of one of the huts, passing through a thick curtain of flies that buzzed in the doorway. Unsaddling his horse, he rubbed it with a handful of dusty straw. When he had finished, he left the shed, saying, "I'll find some water and food for them." Scheherazade nodded, continued grooming the poor old beasts until he returned. The horses ate and drank eagerly, then one after the other tipped up a rear hoof and fell asleep. "Here. Put the saddles and bridles here," he ordered.

"Why do we hide these things?" she asked.

"That is the way things are done in this village," he replied curtly. "These beasts came from here. The villagers expect some payment. Do you have anything of silver or gold to give them?"

Scheherazade took the rings from her ears. "Will these do?"

"Worth more than those nags, but equal to what the villagers will demand." He laughed.

"How did you happen to have horses from this village tethered just where we needed them?" she asked.

"You were not part of my plan. Stealing from the sheikh was. I wanted a mount for my own escape and one on which to carry away a few pieces of his treasure, to pay myself for my captivity. I'd have preferred to take his finest horses, but knew, sadly, that after such a theft he'd surely follow. Unless"—he looked at her closely—"unless you really did kill the old one. Did you?"

"No. He had a fit, cried out in pain, and fell down, then was still. He may indeed be dead."

"So much the better." The ragged fellow spat. "I must now make my way back to my own people. And you? Where will you go?" Without waiting for an answer, he turned and left the stable, saying as he stepped into the sunlight, "Close the door when you come out."

Although she found his habit of issuing orders to her more than a little bit annoying, Scheherazade did close the door, which was a shaky affair made of rope, two tattered skins, and four crooked branches. After two unsuccessful attempts at making it lean into place, Scheherazade tied it shut and made her way outside.

The blazing sun had drained all color, all sound, from an empty world. Only the silent heat shimmered above the ground. That peculiar fellow, her ragged rescuer, strode away from the place in which they had stabled the horses. Scheherazade followed, trying to decide upon some course of action. Should she thank him and go away from this place? But where? Would someone go as a messenger for her? Would this haughty fellow do such service if she asked him? And where was her beloved mare? How on earth had she got into such a mess? How rude that fellow was. Of course, one could not expect someone like that to have good manners.

But what was he, exactly? In the dark, running from the tents of the old sheikh, he had seemed small, a ragged boy. Now, dirty and tattered as he was, he was tall, strong, older than she, and odd. Yes, strange, one minute it seemed clear he was an angry servant, but other times? Peculiar.

Holding her earrings in the palm of his hand, her companion motioned for her to wait outside. He then ducked into the black doorway of one of the huts without first calling out any greeting. Shading her eyes against the sun, Scheherazade looked closely at the other huts. Not a soul in sight, not even a chicken pecking in the dust, not a child making any sound from within. Nothing. What a strange place.

Her companion returned, whistling softly, no sign of the earrings. He must then have left them for the use of the horses. And now?

"We should sleep while we can. A caravan will come before long. For days now, the villagers have been expecting it. Surely it will arrive today. We can leave with that caravan. That is, if you have anything more of value?"

There was her bracelet, of course, but he could not see it, covered as it was by her sleeve. Scheherazade said nothing, made no move to show the bracelet. She had recovered herself somewhat. She would wait to see this caravan. To him, this fellow who stared at her so boldly, she replied, "When the caravan arrives, we can see what they demand."

His response, "As you wish," was delivered with an insolent shrug.

Going into still another hut, again without knocking at the open doorway or calling out any greeting to those who might, in spite of all appearances, be inside, he motioned for her to follow him. After saying that he would return once the caravan arrived, he left the hut.

Scheherazade kicked aside the pile of filthy straw on which he had indicated that she should sleep in that equally squalid hut. Wrapping herself in her cloak, she lay down on what appeared to be the cleanest part of the dirt floor. For a time, she lay awake, growing angrier by the minute. Then did she ask herself a great many questions. Why had she allowed this dirty slave to decide how they would escape? And why had she silently accepted it when he said they could not eat yet? Had he really been a slave to the old sheikh? All the servants, all the horses, everyone she had seen in those few minutes before the tent collapsed, all had been dressed and fed by a great sheikh who cared for his people. Perhaps this fellow was not a prisoner at all but came from this miserable village, a village of thieves. One heard of such places. Had he gone to the old man's tents to steal? Had he saved her from the servants, thinking she might make a hostage, that her family would pay a ransom? His manner? Certainly not humble. Imagine away the dirt and rags, and he would be almost pleasing to the eye, but he was not the one to lead her one step farther. When the caravan arrived, she would bargain with them. She would be fair to him, reward him well once she was home. He could accompany her for the reward or not, as he wished. But she would follow him not one step farther.

In spite of the dirt and heat of that place, she did fall asleep, into a restless, dream-filled sleep . . . a long, long night . . . the sight of that poor old man fallen sick on the carpets of his tent, the terrible mistake his servants made, thinking she would hurt him . . . and that song . . . flute . . . so sad . . . poor old gentleman . . . perhaps he had recovered . . . the flight to this place . . . and what would happen to her beautiful mare?

When she awoke, it was to know that the taste in her mouth was foul, that the hunger in her stomach was painful, and that an insect was walking on her left hand. Sitting up, she shook off the insect, then looked carefully at herself to see if there were more. Satisfied that there were none, she stood up from the floor and brushed off her clothes, combed her hair as best she could with her fingers, and braided it once again. Shaking the dusty straw from her cloak, she put it on, pulling the hood over her head.

Cautiously she peered through the slats at the window. It was nearly dark outside, and there was no one in sight. As she stepped to the doorway, her companion suddenly appeared. He was no longer clothed in rags, but wore instead sturdy, decent garments such as travelers wear. He was the same person he had been before, yet not the same. His eyes shone with excitement, as one who is embarked upon an adventure. He carried a dagger at his waist. The handle of a second peeped from the top of his boot. His face was no longer dirty.

He cut her off from all questions with an abrupt motion for her to keep silent and to come close to the window. "The first riders of the caravan have just arrived," he whispered. "The rest will follow. They are the worst I had feared, smugglers and bandits. We must be careful. . . . They travel to the south, and—"

"No!" whispered Scheherazade fiercely. "I must go home. South will not do. I shall buy some food from them, and a mount, and I shall ride home, or to my great-uncle. . . . No. I'll not go with them. You may if you—"

He bowed to her. "As you wish."

"Are your people to the south?" she added kindly. After all, he had saved her from the sheikh's angry servants.

"No," he replied, "but listen. To the south, just two or three days' journey from here, is the city of Rabazza. There many caravans pass; from there one can journey homeward in safety."

Scheherazade's reply was interrupted by the sounds of camel bells, by the shouts and cries of the caravan. While the two of them watched through the slats of the shutters at the window, the caravan did, with a great deal of cursing and shouting, set up camp. Scheherazade tried to suppress a shudder. Each and every man she saw bore the scars and marks of violence. Some had been branded on the face as criminals. Others had fingers or a hand missing, the usual punishment for theft. All were armed with knives and swords. There seemed to be no slaves, no servants, only men who could be counted on in a fight.

"With such as these . . ." said Scheherazade, throwing back her hood and quickly binding her head and face in the manner of a young man.

"You will consent to travel as my younger brother?"

"With your permission?" she replied.

"To my honor," he said, bending down to remove the small dagger from his boot. "Can you use a knife?"

"Thank you." She nodded. "Mine was in my saddlebag." She tucked the dagger into her belt.

"How can we pay them?" she asked. "I have only this

one bracelet. Honest men I could pay once I have returned home, but they . . . they may decide to sell us as slaves."

"That they will not do. Such as these have not a single slave, not even servants, part of their pride as free criminals. No. I have some things of value. While you slept, I returned to the sheikh's camp." He laughed at her shock. "The old one is recovered from his fit. I could not bring your mare, more's the pity, but I did manage to take saddlebags with food to keep us well."

"Are you a thief, too?" she asked.

"Not really." He laughed again. "After all, they have your mare."

At her look, he added gently, "Ahh. She is well cared for, and not unhappy in the company of the fine horses there. Once you are safely home, you can send for her. After all, these brigands would only steal her from you without even the smile and food I offer."

A tall man, followed by a silent "younger brother," walked out of the hut and asked the nearest of the bandits for permission to travel to Rabazza with their caravan. In reply, the bandit grinned, showing many large yellow teeth, and motioned for them to follow. They were led to the largest of the crew, who did not seem the least surprised at their request. Yes. They could accompany the caravan. Amin would provide them with camels to ride during the four days it would take to reach Rabazza.

"Four days?" asked the tall man. "I was told it was but two days' journey."

"It is four days. You will provide your own food," replied the leader, who turned his back on them without further comment.

For the next two days, Scheherazade was the silent, obedient, "little brother." To the brigands, her companion had called himself Zuphasta. For herself, she was to call him only Elder Brother.

Having agreed to take the two as far as the city of Rabazza, the bandit traders, as they proudly called themselves, then ignored them. It was clear that the brigands felt the two to be no threat, not so much as a pair of fleas.

As they traveled, Scheherazade began to feel a sort of affection for the bandits. True, they were a rough lot, but they prayed as good and obedient men should. Among themselves, they shared without quarrelling, down to the last crumb. While Scheherazade thought her own thoughts and observed their companions from the back of her swaying camel, the one she was to call Elder Brother seemed preoccupied. More than once he muttered that Rabazza could not be more than two and one-half days away from the village. Why had the leader said more? Not knowing the answer, Scheherazade did not make any reply. The two of them ate little, the better to make their food last the full four days of journeying. As they rode, Scheherazade could hear the rumbles of her own stomach, that of the camel, and that of her "elder brother" as well.

On the night after the third day of journeying, Scheherazade dreamed, as she several times had, that she heard once again the flute music, the same sad song that had awakened her at home. How many days ago was that? It seemed forever.

Seeking the music, she awoke. Opening her eyes, she saw that she was in the desert, with the bulky shapes of the camels nearby. Closing her eyes once again, she lay listening. Footsteps quite nearby. Voices. Feigning sleep, she strained to hear what they said.

". . . so hungry," grumbled the first.

"Patience, my friend. You will feast tomorrow night."

"But they are so skinny. We should have fattened them. Just you count their limbs—hardly a morsel for one as famished for human flesh as I am."

"Closer the bone, the sweeter the meat." The second laughed.

There was more said as they walked away, something about Rabazza, and a village to the west, and spices for cooking! How long must she wait until they were out of earshot? How much time before the camp would be awake with no chance for escape?

Scheherazade leaned over her companion. Covering his mouth with her hand, she whispered into his ear. "Wake up. Make no move! Listen!"

His eyes showed white all around before she finished her story. Then he sat up, looked closely at her. "Not a nightmare?" he asked hopefully.

By way of reply, Scheherazade took up her cloak. "The mentioned a village to the west. If we start now, we might make our way there. I'd rather be eaten by the vultures of the desert than by those Ghouls disguised as humans. To think I'd even grown to like them, thinking them bandits who lived by their own rough code, and all the while they were Djiin, Ghouls waiting to crunch our bones and tear at our flesh with their dreadful brass teeth."

"Shhh," her companion urged, "or they will hear the chattering of *our* teeth." Creeping behind the great bulk of the sleeping camels, they stole out of the camp, past the outlying guard asleep at his post.

"Confident devils to sleep so sweetly while on guard," whispered her companion after they were safely out of hearing.

For the rest of the night and for the cool part of the morning, they kept up a good pace, always walking westward. They saw not a glimpse of the village; but, at the top of a rise, in the clear early light, there were in the distance immense mountains, with tips gleaming white. "In that place," said her companion, "the snows never melt, even when small flowers bloom in the cracks and crevices of the great boulders."

"You have been there?" asked Scheherazade.

"Yes." He nodded. Without another word, he started down the rise. As they continued westward, he went in silence, though the line between his brows showed clearly that his thoughts were troubled.

As the sun grew hot, they wrapped their eyes against the glare, pulled their hoods far over their faces, and walked without speaking. The one she now called, even to herself, Elder Brother continually altered his place as he went, so that his taller shadow should fall on her to give her what relief he could from the sun.

Scheherazade, for her part, was listening to an argument between her head and her stomach. The head said that she should be a child of the desert as she once had been. She certainly could go for long days and nights with little food and water. Her head accused her whole body of having grown soft during the time she had lived in cities. She should be ashamed of her softness, her head insisted. The stomach replied by attempting to count exactly how many days it had been since some food of any quantity or quality had come its way. The stomach protested that the day and night with the baby elephant had not been times of feasting, and that not so long since, they had fasted for one whole month, and that everyone should pity poor stomach and feed it. To still both stomach and head, Scheherazade began to hum the song the flute had played in her dreams and in the palace so many days ago. Her companion seemed not to hear. Pity, thought Scheherazade, if he has no ear for music, but has so many other good qualities.

In this way, they walked on until even the humming failed to make her throat forget the heat, and Scheherazade, too, fell silent.

After a time, he stopped. "Please," he said, "when my mouth is not so dry, do remind me to tell you a story, the one the old man mentioned."

"You know it? The tale of the . . . something."

"Reluctant Bethrothéd Pair," he supplied. "Yes. I heard it in the old man's tents." He stared absently past her in the direction from which they had come.

Scheherazade, caught between her companion's gloom and her own hunger, lowered her eyes. There it was, at their feet, the clear signs, a path! Without flagging, they followed it until they could see, shimmering in the heat, the white houses and tall palms of an oasis, the village.

chapter Three

T*wo strangers approached a village that lay waiting* for the midday heat to pass. Not even a dog raised its head at their coming. It was the time when everyone with good sense was somewhere, in the coolest shade to be found, asleep.

At last, one small boy playing a game with stones and pegs looked out from the shadows and greeted them. After returning the greeting, the taller of the strangers asked who in the village had a kind heart toward weary and hungry travelers.

"Almost everyone," replied the boy, "except the old man who lives over there." He rolled his head and eyes toward a certain house in the next street. "He is so stingy that his poor old wife has long since died sad and childless. He, begrudging the very air a slave or servant would need, lives entirely alone. I doubt there is even a fly to be found in his house." The boy spat. "That one gives away only slaps and curses—and those he uses twice!"

When the strangers laughed, the boy looked pleased; but then, most puzzled when the taller stranger turned and walked directly toward the old man's dwelling. "They'll be sorry," the boy muttered, returning to his game.

"Why," whispered Scheherazade, for she was the smaller of the two strangers, still in her disguise as Younger Brother, "why do we go to the one he warned us against?"

"Because there we can eat very well, and I can give the old man a gift," replied Elder Brother, who had already begun to knock at the house door.

After a time, someone appeared, one eye squinting at them through a hole in the door.

"The blessings of Allah be upon you," Elder Brother greeted him.

The old man's response came muffled through the thick door. Scheherazade rather doubted it was a blessing. Nevertheless, the old one did not leave them standing there but listened when Elder Brother continued.

"We are two travelers who ask that we be permitted to cook for you a most delicious supper!"

At this, a small window in the door was opened.

"We have brought everything necessary to cook this wonderful meal for you, honored one. We ask only that you join us for the eating of it."

"You have food?"

"Indeed."

The old man looked astonished, then suspicious. "Supper?"

"Yes," said Elder Brother. "We will prepare for you a meal such as you have never before tasted, a meal to bring comfort to you."

"I have no money for such extravagances!" shouted the old one, moving away from the small window in the door.

"We ask nothing!" insisted Elder Brother, "only your company for the eating."

The old man rubbed the whiskers of his chin, peered intently out at them. "Comfort? And you have all the food for this meal?" he asked.

"We would"—Elder Brother smiled—"do well to have use, and only the use, of one of your soup pots for the cooking. Naturally, we'll return it to you beautifully scrubbed and polished when you have finished the eating of its glorious contents."

"That is all you need? A pot? Why have you no pot?" asked the old man.

"A pot to use for this one meal is our need," replied Elder Brother. "Ours was unfortunately stolen from us when last we did a kindness for one who, may Allah forgive him, took advantage of us. We are merely humble servants of Allah, on a pilgrimage to thank Allah for the special blessing he has bestowed upon us."

His face close against the small window in the door, the old man repeated. "A soup pot? You have everything else for a meal that I shall eat?"

"Indeed." Elder Brother's smile was reassuring. "Thanks be to Allah."

"To Him," muttered the old man. "Then hand me the knife from your belt, and yours as well, young fellow! You shall not enter my house bearing weapons against me!"

Without enthusiasm, Scheherazade relinquished her small dagger to the old man. He stared hard at her as if to discover some hidden weapon. Elder Brother raised his arms to show he bore neither weapons nor ill will toward the old man.

Slowly the door opened just wide enough for them to enter. For a moment, the old man's face softened a bit, nearly smiled. And Scheherazade, looking from Elder Brother to the old man and back again, was amazed. How charming Elder Brother's smile. How white his teeth. How his eyes sparkled with affection. How well he could pretend, and move as if he had been raised a prince and not the dirty, ragged lout he had seemed when they met. Strange.

Elder Brother led Scheherazade inside. "Yes, Uncle. You see, my little brother and I have something truly wonderful to cook for you." They waited while the old man closed and bolted the door, then followed him into the kitchen.

"Now." Elder Brother rubbed his hands briskly together, looking around the place, which was tidy and quite bare. "First. Little Brother, go to fetch water from the well for our soup."

At Scheherazade's look, he continued in the coaxing tone an affectionate older brother uses toward a much younger one. "Go, go, go. Run! so that we can cook."

The old man pointed to his water jugs, then unbolted the kitchen door and pointed toward the village well. As she left, she could hear him close and bolt the door behind her. Scheherazade went to the well. When she returned, the old man opened the door as she approached, then bolted it once more behind her.

While Scheherazade put the water jug in its place, the old man took out a huge ring of keys. Selecting one, he opened a cupboard and hauled from it a cooking pot large enough to bathe a baby. Scheherazade took up the jug once again and poured water into the pot.

"Now." Elder Brother sighed. "To feast." He put his right hand into the folds of his shirt and brought forth a small leather bag. From the bag, he took five large pebbles, pebbles of a dazzling white, as if moonlight shone on them while they lay in the bed of a swiftly moving stream. Elder Brother held them up and sighed again.

"These will give us our soup."

"Those white pebbles?" asked the old man.

"See, and then smell it once it simmers," was the reply. Opening his hand over the pot, he dropped two white pebbles into the water.

Sighing, the old man sat down on a low stool, put his two hands on his two knees, and stared at the pot.

After he had settled the pot onto the hottest part of the stove, Elder Brother put two, four, six, eight more pebbles into the water!

"Now," he said, "while we wait for the wonderful aroma to tickle our noses, we must replenish Uncle's water supply. Go, Little Brother, to bring more water."

Gritting her teeth, Scheherazade picked up the larger of the water jugs and handed it to Elder Brother, looking up at him as a worshipful little brother would to a big, strong, elder brother.

"Help me?" she asked in her best little brother voice.

With a kindly smile, he took the large jug. Scheherazade took the smaller one. Elder Brother unbolted the kitchen door. As they walked away, they could hear the old man bolt it once again behind them.

"Will he let us in again?" asked Scheherazade.

"He is greedy," replied Elder Brother.

When they returned with the water, the old man gave them a thin smile. "Truly it begins to simmer, and truly there is a desirable aroma." He nodded his old head, "It is one to make your mouth water."

"Indeed." Elder Brother smiled. He tasted the contents of the pot. The old man leaned forward on his stool.

"There are some"—Elder Brother tilted his head to one side as if debating with himself—"there are some who like a bit more salt in their food."

The old man took the spoon from Elder Brother's hand, filled it with broth, blew loudly on the contents, then sipped noisily. Putting down the spoon, he fetched a bowl of salt from a locked cupboard. Adding first a small pinch, he squinted at Elder Brother, then added a second, larger one.

The smells that came from the pot grew stronger as the water began to boil. Scheherazade pushed her stomach with her fist to still its growls. She did not need the smell of food to make her mouth water.

"Here now, Uncle. Care to taste it?" Elder Brother offered the spoon once again to the old man.

Nodding his head, the old one took the spoon. With one long slurp, he drained the contents, closed his eyes.

"Although it is *excellent,*" said Elder Brother, "a—"

"Bit of carrot!" interjected the old man.

"Yes . . . indeed," as if it were a new and wonderful notion.

Bringing out a large carrot from still another locked closet, the old man closed his eyes once more. "And maybe—though it is very good—maybe an onion."

"Excellent," agreed Elder Brother, cutting the carrot into the soup, followed quickly by the onion.

The three of them watched the pot in silence for the time it took for the carrot and the onion to add their odor to the delicious smells that came from the pot. The old man had resumed his place on the low stool.

"Aha!" cried the old man.

Scheherazade and Elder Brother jumped at the sound.

"A piece of laurel leaf would do it well." His eyes glittered as he spoke.

"Agreed." Elder Brother sighed, and the laurel leaf was added.

"Pepper?" suggested Elder Brother, when next the old man tasted the liquid.

The pepper was added.

Upon the next tasting, Elder Brother suggested that perhaps the flavor lacked the nuance one could provide by adding a single clove, although there were those who disputed such refinements.

The old man, accepting a spoonful of broth to confirm or reject this opinion, grunted what must have been agreement, for he brought out from another locked cupboard a clove, which naturally had to be stuck into another onion, which also was added to the pot.

All the while Scheherazade had not been given a single taste of the broth. All the while she struggled with the hunger that consumed her stomach. After a time, she smiled at Elder Brother as she sauntered over to the pot and took a good long sniff of the air above the simmering broth.

"A hen?" she suggested.

Elder Brother stifled a gasp, then immediately struck his right fist upon his left palm with a loud smack. "You were *ever* so!" he cried. "What a suggestion! You know nothing of cooking!"

"I know of eating!" Scheherazade shouted, in her best angry little brother voice.

"No!" Elder Brother rejoined. "No hen into *my* soup."

"I'm not suggesting you ruin it by adding a miserable dry old bone, with hardly a shred of meat," insisted Scheherazade, "but a fat hen."

At this, the old man stood up from his stool and marched toward the pot. Scheherazade stepped back. The old man grabbed the spoon from her hand, tasted, glared at both of them, then snatched up a large knife in one hand. Dropping the spoon onto the table, he took up a small bowl. "Open the door and come with me," he ordered.

Scheherazade unbolted the door and followed the old man out of the kitchen into the back courtyard, leaving the door open behind them.

In no time at all, they were back, with Scheherazade, as the youngest of the three, assigned the task of plucking the hen, which the old man had caught and dispatched in the twinkling of an eye, clean of every single pinfeather. While she worked, the old man unlocked still another cupboard and took out a wooden platter upon which lay the remains of a leg of lamb. Bone and hen went into the pot.

Then and only then did the old man speak. "You were both wrong! And wrong to quarrel! But"—he shook his finger at Scheherazade—"especially you were wrong to criticize your elder brother." With this, the old man sat back down on his stool to watch the pot.

After the next tasting, Elder Brother closed his eyes to think. The old man took the spoon from his hand and dipped it into the soup. He tasted and said, "Little Brother, bring a sprig of parsley from the garden."

This done, out came the keys, and a cupboard was unlocked. From it, the old man added to the soup two big handfuls of barley and one of lentils. Frowning, pursing his lips as if faced with some terrible decision, he then reached his great hand into a sack of rice. That, too, was added to the pot.

After a time, Scheherazade was permitted to taste the broth. Unfortunately, that taste, and the heavenly smells that filled the kitchen, only made her feel the pains of her hunger with greater intensity. She watched as if in a dream while the old man brought wooden bowls and spoons and set them upon the table. Alongside the bowls, he put some bread.

At last, Elder Brother said, "I believe the magic white pebbles have done their work." He offered the spoon to the old man.

Carefully, the old one blew on the broth, sipped it loudly, smacked his lips, slurped again. After a moment, he rubbed his greasy chin. "Yes. They have done their work. It is truly a soup fit for the Caliph."

"Uncle." Elder Brother smiled and bowed. "May we invite you to supper?"

Indeed. They could. The old man sat himself down on one stool, indicated that Elder Brother should sit to his right and Scheherazade, the Little Brother, at the end of the table. The old one said the blessing, which was brief and to the point.

They ate and ate, and then they ate some more. Soon a pile of clean bones filled a wooden platter. The old man dipped again and again into the pot. Again and again he emptied his bowl, and again and again he belched contentedly, but still he dipped the big spoon into the pot. At last, he looked deep into the pot and cried out in disappointment. "Ahhgghh. Your magic white pebbles. Only one remains!"

"No matter," replied Elder Brother. "That one is good for a simple meal." He took the single pebble from the pot and carefully wiped it clean and white. "I have more, enough here in my bag for five meals, ten if one is thrifty." He pulled forth the leather bag, and sure enough, there were ten more large, beautiful, white pebbles shining in the light of the kitchen lamp.

"Ahh. For travelers, that is good." The old man sighed, lowering his eyes, from which the greed glittered in the lamplight. Then he rose from his place and walked slowly, as one does who has eaten a great deal. From a cupboard, he brought to the table a handful of dates, of which the old man ate the greater part.

"This magic," said Elder Brother, accepting the old man's offer of a few dates, "was given to me by a great Djinn. When I am not traveling, I must bury them, each and every one in its own special and secret place in the garden, so that when the moon shines they can recapture the light and the magic thereof. If it is the will of Allah, these pebbles will keep me all my life long. Thanks be to Allah."

"Praise be," replied the old man. When he had stood up from the table, he pointed out the back door. "I had a mind—because your magic pebbles did give me supper—to let you sleep in my house. But"—he shook his finger at them—"you did not quite fulfill your promise. I provided the bread and the dates for our supper. Still, I am forgiving, and so you two may sleep in my shed and be well on your way tomorrow in the cool before the sun. Ah, yes, and your own weapons you will find beside the door when you depart."

Thanking and blessing the old one, the two travelers went to their rest in the shed.

It was during the night that Scheherazade thought that perhaps she dreamed that the old man came in the moonlight, with a knife at his waist, and took the leather sack from beneath her companion's head and crept away with it.

In the morning, Elder Brother told her it had been no dream. And he laughed. "The old man will bury them in the garden, and he will forget one, or misplace it, no matter how he tries, for there are twelve and not ten pebbles in that sack, and two of the twelve are double. And of them all, one is indeed a white pebble from the streams of the great mountains. And the rest are something like onions, but not onions, and they truly are magic. Once in the ground, they will grow and flower and bear seeds that will blow in the wind. And when they grow, the boys of the village will steal from him. For misers teach the boys that whatever the miser has is secret and is of value, and misers teach that what the miser has can only be got by theft. And then"—he laughed again—"the whole village can enjoy soups made from the white pebbles, thanks be to Allah and the miser He uses for His work."

chapter four

Ahead of them lay the desert, soft in the light before dawn; behind them, the village, where the talk at the well had been encouraging. Word had it among the villagers that Bedouins were camped one or two days' journey from the village. Upon being told which clan it was, Scheherazade wanted to sing for joy. These were people known, cousins of cousins. Now, at last, she and her companion could make their way home. Straight from the well they set out, walking in the direction they had been told.

"Allah be praised," sang Scheherazade as they left the village far behind them. "We have been so fortunate that we have escaped the anger of the sheikh's servants, have not been eaten by the bandits who were *Ghouls,* and have ourselves eaten gloriously well with the old miser last night. The water from the village well this morning was cold and sweet, and if it be the will of Allah, we shall soon find ourselves together with family and friends."

"To His Name," her companion replied, speaking far more quietly than Scheherazade had expected. What had made him so gloomy? From beneath her lashes, she looked sidewise at him. He stared down at the ground at his feet.

"What is this brooding?" she continued. "You did promise to tell me a story once you had a throat not parched into silence."

"Pardon?" One single word, and he was again silent and distant. How could his whole manner be so different from the bossy, confident, and dirty youth who had pulled her from the tent? Scheherazade looked away from him, studied instead the path before her.

They walked in this way for several hours, until that one she had called Elder Brother so lost himself in his thoughts that he stumbled. Upon recovering his footing, he sighed.

"Where are your thoughts?" she asked after some time had passed.

He sighed again. "Turning on themselves. True, we have survived these past days and we do walk toward friends, but so much happened that was not . . ." He broke off, shook himself, and continued in quite a different tone. "Yes. I had promised you the story the old sheikh promised . . . a story too appropriate. . . ." And for the third time he sighed. . . .

There were once two cousins, he began, fearless and generous in their youth, cousins devoted to one another. They did swear before the birth of their first children that the two to be born would be as brothers if boys, sisters if girls, and that if one should have a son and the other a daughter, the two would be wed to one another to make the love these two cousins bore for one another into a family of many generations—if it would be the will of Allah.

And as it happened, one became the father of a fine son, the other of a fine daughter. The two children were as beautiful as the light, as strong and joyful as two young colts. They had spirit, generosity, beauty, all that fathers' hearts desire in their children.

The two fathers, though they had been richly blessed by Allah with flocks and rich tents, with tellers of tales and singers of songs, with all that could satisfy the stomach and the eye, had not grown in wisdom as they had grown in age. The two fathers looked around them at the peace and prosperity of their tents and lamented that the life their children led was a life that lacked the excitement, the danger, the romance of the days when they had themselves been young. The two old men imagined that in their youth the world had been more vibrant, more worthy.

"Where"—they sighed to one another—"where in all these dull days are the many raids? Why do not the young men ride off more often to plunder the rich herds of camels that belong to a foe befitting the family? Why do not the women more often cheer their men into battle?"

"The men must ride!" insisted the old ones. "And as they ride, the women—filling the air with high-pitched trills—the women must loose their long black hair to be lifted and tossed by the wind as they stand on the hill outside camp!"

Thus, the old ones disparaged the life of the present day and longed for a past remembered as golden.

And the daughter and son? They grew to be as perfect as any father could desire, perfect in all ways except one. And in that one, they were as foolish as their fathers. This boy and this girl, so full of spirit and generosity, felt only irritation with one another. They began to quarrel as babies, before they could properly speak. Year by year, the disputes between them did not grow fewer. No, indeed. Although each of them was as beautiful, as desirable as the sweet song of a bird, not music, but sparks flew between them as between two flinty stones!

As the time approached to wed the two who were

betrothed to one another, the girl pleaded with her father. "No, please, dear father. Marry me to any man in the world but that one! Please!"

And likewise, the son with his father insisted, "Father, marry me to any shrew, any she-devil in the world save that one. Food and water are bitter in her presence! Spare me, Father!"

Faced with these children, what did the fathers do?

Instead of bringing their young son and daughter together in marriage, if it should be the will of Allah, the two fathers decided to bring this most reluctant betrothéd pair together through an adventure.

At first, the fathers thought to have the bride kidnapped. Honor would demand that her promised bridegroom go to rescue her. But, no, the fathers feared the stubborn girl might refuse his rescue. And they feared that the stubborn groom might ride off to go hunting rather than to save his intended bride. Over many and then many more tiny cups of sweet thick coffee, the two fathers plotted and planned, and finally agreed. The bethrothed pair should *both* be kidnapped and held captive in the same place together. In their struggle to free themselves, they would forget their differences, and the fathers could savor it all: the adventure, the escape of the pair, and the joy of the marriage.

In secret, the fathers engaged trusted retainers to act as kidnappers, all to be done in utmost secrecy and in disguise so complete that none should recognize them. And so it came about that the girl was sitting with her sisters one day at their weaving. All the men and boys, even to the very last one, had gone off with horse and hawk to hunt. The women and girls were alone in the camp when fierce, armed strangers came and carried off the girl.

That very same day, while he saddled the favorite stallion of his father, the reluctant bridegroom was set upon by ten men and carried off, bound hand and foot, into a place of concealment that was far, far from the tents of home.

There, in that secret place, the girl found herself separated by the inner wall of a tent from another, one she heard groaning and struggling at the ropes that bound him hand and foot.

"Hsst," said the girl to the cloth wall against which her face was pressed.

Looking about in the darkness, making certain he was truly alone, the boy answered the voice at his back. "Is someone there? Are you also a bound prisoner?"

"Yes," whispered the girl, "although my feet are but loosely tied. I can perhaps free them."

"If so," replied the boy, "then perhaps you can lift the cloth that separates us. Are your hands bound before you or behind?"

"Before," said the girl, "but tied to my waist, so that I cannot bite at the ropes."

"We can help one another," said the boy, "for mine are bound behind. If you untie me, then I can untie you."

Freeing her feet, which had been left in that manner just so that the two could untie themselves, the girl worked to raise the fabric of the inner wall.

While the two struggled to free themselves, their mothers, believing the children kidnapped, wailed and tore their hair. The two fathers, who had vowed not to tell anyone of the great plan, tried to restore calm, all the while longing to learn how the reluctant bethrothéd pair were faring, wishing to be mice in the tent and thus to savor the success of the undertaking.

And while they wished, and while the poor mothers wept, the news of the kidnapping spread through the encampments of the desert like wildfire. And like wildfire, it inflamed all who were touched by the story. Far and wide, all the members of the clan raced for their horses, raced to follow the trail of the kidnappers with swords drawn and eyes ablaze.

In the darkened tent, in those long minutes it took for the two prisoners to reach through the opening at the bottom of the tent wall—during the time of groping for ropes to untie first the girl's hands, then the boy's bounds—in those minutes the two spoke together, whispered encouragements. In their talk, in the dark, the did not recognize one another. In their talk, in the dark, they wondered who had kidnapped them and why.

"Perhaps," said the girl, "it is the answer to my many prayers that I be spared an evil that was to befall me."

"Perhaps," replied the boy, who found the sounds of her voice so pleasing to his ear, and the imagining of her person so pleasing to his heart. "Perhaps I, too, will somehow be spared the fate I did dread."

As the prisoners whispered and worked against the bonds, the fathers rode hard to reach the hiding place, but rode not more swiftly than did the clansmen set on raiding the kidnappers, set on taking revenge for the kidnapping.

The prisoners spoke, and they pried loose the binding knots, and then worked to make the opening large enough for one of them to crawl through. Once the opening would be large enough, they could be together in the same part of the tent, prisoners in the dark. "Soon," they whispered to one another, "soon we can be together, and plan our further escape."

Ah. At last. The opening was large enough for the girl, slender and supple as a green willow wand, to slip through. The boy held out his hand to help her to her feet.

At that touch, in the space of breathing out and breathing in, the two felt a love for one another that made them sigh with one voice.

Then, from the sigh sprang surprised laughter when their eyes, now long accustomed to the secret darkness of the tent, saw and recognized one another.

Then the two felt a brief moment of shame at their past quarrelsomeness. "The will of Allah," they whispered to one another. In joy, they thought to face that small problem, that they must seek their freedom.

But, no! The clansmen, swords flashing, horses neighing, thundered up to the tents and fell upon the loyal retainers disguised as kidnappers! Sword rang against sword. Cries filled the night!

And in the bloody fight that ensued, the no longer reluctant bethrothéd pair, those once-defiant children, were slain. And the foolish fathers did arrive to see the many bloody dead and to tear out their beards in shame and sorrow.

"May we listen for the will of Allah and follow his way," whispered Scheherazade.

"Praise be to his name," replied her companion.

chapter five

The smell of cooking food. No, not imagined. Scheherazade had not thought once of food that whole long day of walking. No. It was most certainly the smell of food, of cooking fires, followed—after they had taken a few steps more—by what were surely the faint sounds of bells. There it was, clear on the evening air, the tinkling of small bells on goats, the deeper tones of the larger ones on camels.

And then, there it was, the whole encampment, and then the greetings. At last, she was no longer a stranger alone. Here was family! Everyone greeting her. She, here on foot, and no word had they heard of her coming! Then she turned to make her companion known to them, red faced that she knew not his true name, nor anything of his people, and wondered if he would be ashamed. But he had shown neither fear nor surprise when they had set out for this camp. Surely these, her people, were not his enemies. Why, then, when she turned back to call him forward, why was he gone? And where? And how?

When all her questions about him were met with blank looks, or with looks as questioning as her own, Scheherazade wondered about her own mind. Was this one she had called Elder Brother then a Djinn? Had she imagined a companion to still the fears that arose in her own heart? Greatly puzzled, she stayed with these, her kinfolk, until she could travel home, not alone this time, but with her own people.

Her mare, she learned, had, most mysteriously, already been delivered back to her home, with messages to reassure all the family that she was well and safe and that she would return after she had made some visits in the desert. Most mysterious. Who had sent such messages? No mention was made of the white-haired sheikh. Was he, too, a Djinn?

Greatly troubled, Scheherazade returned home, traveling this time on horseback, with enough to eat and drink, surrounded by those who loved her. And yet, she discovered that she missed that strange fellow, wondered where he was and how he fared—wondered if he had been a human after all. Although there were many questions she would have asked of him, what she missed, to her great surprise, was the easy quiet in which they had traveled together. No. She had not particularly noticed it as they journeyed, only now that he was gone forever.

On the last night of her homeward journey, Scheherazade was awakened once again by the sound of a flute. It played the melody she had heard that last night at home, the one of which she had dreamed so often. When, next morning, she asked, others said they had heard it, praised the melody, but no one knew who had made music while they slept.

At home once again, Scheherazade said no word to correct what all the family believed, that she had been making visits, listening to stories, stories she would, in time, tell to them. And tell she did, a story about magic white pebbles and the soup they made. She told another, about the reluctant bethrothéd pair, which made everyone weep and sigh.

To a casual visitor, it might have seemed that all was as it had been in Scheherazade's small palace. In truth, even the birds living in the garden could have told the visitor a different story. True, Scheherazade worked as she had, teaching those who came to her. She prayed, and she fasted as she should. She read, but rarely sang. She was there, but she was not there.

* * *

"Ahh," said Auntie Berthe, not for the first time since the girl had returned. "There you are again, lost in some dream."

"I was thinking," said Scheherazade, "that I should like to travel to the far mountains. Do you know that it is always cold in that place? There is snow even when the small flowers bloom from cracks within huge boulders."

"Ahh, child. It's not travel you need."

"Nor to be married, Auntie. I know the song you sing." Scheherazade laughed and began to hum the melody played by the flute that night. "If you continue to press me, I'll agree as a dutiful girl must, but as a Princess I shall say that I'll have only the mysterious one who plays that melody."

"Sstt! Stubborn child. Don't say that. What if the one who makes that music is old, toothless? Never make such foolish promises!"

"But then I'd be married, and you would be happy at least."

"No, dear child. I meant only that you do not sigh for travel to far and cold places."

"Certainly I do not sigh for a person, real or imagined, to marry, or for the married life I could have if I put myself in your hands."

"Ah, child. A Princess is cut off from most suitors.

Her family can find the best one, far better than she can."

"No one has found the one who plays the flute," Scheherazade responded.

"You did not even inquire if there had been word from the so handsome, so mysterious sender of gifts to all of us," said the old woman, changing her approach.

"Ah," said the girl, "that one. He was not here to win me as a wife . . . to win all of you perhaps."

"Then you have seen something or someone during your travels!" The old woman, giving her a sudden, crafty glance, whispered close to the girl's ear.

"No, darling Auntie," replied Scheherazade, giving the old woman a hug. "No. You will have no one else but me to order around from the dark before dawn until the dark before sleep."

All of that day, and of the next, and of the day that followed, Scheherazade sat bent over maps. She studied the mountains she had seen in the distance, maps of mountains near and far.

Thus preoccupied, Scheherazade took little notice of the many whispered conferences that took place during those days. She did not observe that preparations were being made to entertain guests of great importance. When summoned, she appeared for meals but ate with an absentminded air.

Thus it was that she was nudged rather forcefully by her Auntie Berthe one day. Looking as she had been directed, Scheherazade was somewhat surprised to see, seated there in the place of honor beside her eldest brother, a certain visitor, one she never had expected to see.

That the others in the household were not surprised was also quite obvious to her. All of them gazed upon the visitor with pleasure, but—how interesting—with none of the feverish excitement his first visit had brought with it. True, he was himself somewhat changed. His black beard was longer now, and his hair, which had reached to his shoulders, was shorter now, curling on his neck. He was more somber.

"The blessings of Allah be upon you and upon this house," the mysterious stranger, giver of baby elephants, said, bowing low. He was quieter, without the extravagant flourishes that had marked his speech upon his previous visit.

"And upon you," she replied. Still, she had to be cautious. What was being plotted here?

Yes, the visitor was much changed in his manner. He subjected them to no monologue; indeed, he was most often silent.

Scheherazade, however, kept herself on guard for the time when the meal would be finished. He was the one, after all, who had put her household into tumult with his gifts. What, she wondered, did he have planned for them now?

After the meal, the guest bowed low to Scheherazade. "Princess," he began.

Scheherazade noticed the melting of eyes to hear him speak. She herself felt no such softening.

"Princess. Please forgive me for my conduct during my previous visit. The disturbances to your household were, I confess, deliberate."

At this, even Scheherazade started.

"Yes. It was my purpose to disrupt so completely your household that you would flee, alone, into the desert for refuge and solitude."

Scheherazade remained silent, hoping this time that the formerly long-winded guest would tell her more.

Instead, he bowed deeply, called many blessings upon all of them, and backed out of the room, bowing repeatedly. He said only, as he stood at the door, "It was done out of . . ." His voice dropped so low that she could not catch every word. ". . . will come to tell you more."

Gone. The visitor was gone, having once again left the palace buzzing very much like a hive of bees into which someone has thrown a stone.

More amazed than annoyed, Scheherazade went to her chamber, where neither thoughts nor dreams gave her any clue to the meaning of the stranger's actions.

Even Auntie Berthe had little to say, except that there would be a second visitor, soon.

All the next day Scheherazade ignored the maps, forced herself to attend only to the household accounts, using columns of numbers to force out of her head the questions she could not answer.

Indeed, that evening there was another visitor, one truly unexpected. There stood a man, tall and straight, hawklike eyes fierce beneath snow-white brows, beard and hair of like white, long, long beard and hair, long fingers on strong hands. He bowed a return to her greeting.

"Thanks be to Allah for your good health," said Scheherazade.

Then, as before, the guest and the family ate and drank together, meanwhile conversing easily on many subjects. All, that is, but Scheherazade, who was silent. No one remarked on it, as it was seemly for a young woman to listen to her elders, even a princess, especially when the elder came as a great sheikh of the desert.

Scheherazade had told no one in the family how she had met the sheikh that night in the desert, how he had invited her to be his guest, how he had collapsed, crying out in pain, nor how she had been attacked by his servants.

When the meal was ended, the sheikh rose from his place, then made a deep bow to each of them, last of all to Scheherazade. Greatly amazed, the whole company fell silent. Then, taking his white beard and his hair in both hands, the sheikh pulled them from his head. Slowly he peeled the fierce white eyebrows from above his eyes. Each movement he made was accompanied by gasps of surprise from the servants, who stood frozen in the acts of pouring, or raising or lowering platters.

"Please forgive me, Princess," he said, once again bowing low.

Seeing him, hearing him, and still not believing, no one spoke. There, beneath the white beard and hair, without the bristling snow-white eyebrows, there stood the man they had known until this moment as the mysterious visitor, the giver of lavish gifts, the one who had confessed to having visited them solely to disrupt their household. He, the very one over whom all the maidens in the household had sighed. How could he also be the old sheikh of the desert? And why?

"I took this disguise, Princess, as . . . please forgive me . . ."

Once again the visitor, still bowing low, backed away to the door and departed from their presence.

"This has been most strange, most astonishing. Do you understand it?" asked her eldest brother.

"No," said Scheherazade. While the others discussed these bewildering events, she excused herself, and said good-night, and went to her room.

"There is"—sighed Auntie Berthe—"yet another visitor to come—tomorrow. Perhaps then we shall know the meaning of . . . of—"

"This truly is not a plot fashioned by your very own mind and hands?" asked Scheherazade skeptically.

"Truly."

"I do believe," said Scheherazade, "that I know the person of the next visitor."

"You do?"

"I believe I do. But although it is a straight line from the first visitor to the sheikh to that person, I cannot imagine why."

"And will you be pleased to see this person?" Auntie Berthe spoke slowly, her look sly.

"Perhaps."

"Praise be." The old woman sighed. "Now, here's your good-night kiss. Sleep."

Scheherazade lay back upon the pillows. Auntie Berthe chuckled and whispered, fussing over the hang of each and every curtain, the position of a branch of blossoms in a vase, until at last she was satisfied and went, with one last sigh, to her own rest.

chapter Six

The following morning Scheherazade rose early from her couch. After prayers, she went into the garden and called them to her, all the ones who had come to hear and to tell the stories of many times and places. Bringing their work, they came to sit together in the garden. One after another, a voice took up the telling, while needles led brightly colored threads in and out of cloth. Above them, the trees swayed and whispered as small birds hopped from branch to branch, eating and singing. The voices of the tellers rose and fell, accompanied by the trickling of water dripping into the basin of the fountain, the soft click of the looms, the rustle of shelling and husking.

After the midday meal, they went to rest. Scheherazade had not told the story of the old sheikh, nor any other, that morning, although the others would have listened most willingly.

The first to arise from their afternoon rest were the cooks and kitchen helpers. The gatekeeper, who might well have slept longer, was awakened by a knocking. He opened the window to see standing there, holding the bridle of his horse like any other traveler, a face he knew, even when that face was covered against the sun and wind. Opening the gates wide, the gatekeeper bowed low, then quickly summoned his wife. "Run!" he cried. "Tell the Princess who is here."

"Welcome." Scheherazade bowed to the visitor.

"Ahh. Princess Storyteller, for many long months I have not heard any tales told by Scheherazade. Riding now, in disguise, through the kingdom to observe for myself how my government treats my people, I decided to give myself a reward. May I taste the food of your cooks and listen to the tales told in your household?"

"It is our honor and our pleasure," replied Scheherazade.

The lamps had been lit, the cooks praised, and the family and guests made comfortable on their cushions. The promised third visitor had not arrived. The evening breeze stirred the curtains and caused the palm fronds to sway. The scent of orange blossoms was pleasing even to ones who waited and wondered.

Expectantly, the Sultan turned to Scheherazade and said, "And now, Princess, tell us. . . ."

With a low bow to her guests, Scheherazade began. There once was, if there ever was, a Princess who lived in a far-off kingdom, where, from her bedroom window, the snow-capped mountains looked close enough to touch. A mysterious visitor came one day to the gates of her house. . . .

Her telling ended with the words the visitor had spoken in that very room just one short day ago.

"*And?*" said the Sultan. "And what did the third visitor have to say to them?"

Then, as Scheherazade's eldest brother looked perplexed, as Eldest Brother rubbed his beard and Scheherazade gave what may have been a sigh, from the garden came music—a flute, played by one whose heart came out in liquid notes. It was a song Scheherazade knew well.

The Sultan closed his eyes, the better to hear. Scheherazade, however, tried very hard to see who it was standing in the shadows within the garden.

When the song was ended, no one stirred. After a time, the Sultan spoke. "Please, Princess, call the player into the light that we may reward such beauty."

"That one is shy," she replied, "and may already have run away." Rising from her place, she went to the garden. Perhaps he had gone, and she would never know how or why or what.

But, no. There he was. Bowing low, he came toward her. He followed her into the light.

"This is the one the bandit Ghouls in the story were told to call Zuphasta, which was not his true name, the one the Princess in the story called Elder Brother.

"And it was he," said the Sultan, delighted, "he who made the music and the soup that stole the heart of the Princess! Ahh, Princess Scheherazade. You have devised a most wonderful entertainment for me! And yet you say that my visit was a surprise!" He chuckled with pleasure. The whole family joined in his laughter, all but Scheherazade and the stranger.

"And now," said the Sultan, "can we hear how the tale ends?"

Scheherazade returned to her seat. A place was made for the visitor, food and drink placed before him.

"Yes! Yes!" cried the Sultan. "Drink. Eat. You deserve richer rewards even than the excellence this household offers. But all that in good time. First you must slake your thirst. You must eat."

Here the Sultan paused, dropped his voice to a whisper, and leaning forward, said, There came to my palace, not so very long ago, a most curious visitor from a country beyond the mountains and seas. Years and the fierce winds of desert, mountain, and sea had sucked from him all youth. Toothless, sightless, he travels still, though he seems barely more alive than the gnarled stick upon which he leans. When he speaks, however, all else falls away, as if Life itself were a dream. This visitor told me of a merchant who lived in the land we call India, a rich merchant living a life of exquisite opulence. The merchant had a terrible weakness, a wife he adored. Her weakness was that she loved best whatever love was nearest. Knowing her frailty, and his own jealousy, the merchant stayed close by his wife's side. And, indeed, together they were happy.

Then, in time, during which the merchant's love for his wife had not lessened, the merchant's business absolutely demanded his attention. He had to travel away from his fickle, oh, so beautiful wife. But what could he do? How could he keep her safely at home, alone, while he traveled?

Desperate, the merchant put off his fine clothes and walked, unattended, barefoot and in the ragged garments of a pentitent, out of the city and into the foothills, where there lived a holy man, ancient of the ancients, sitting under a tree praying for all living creatures.

When the merchant arrived, prepared to wait until

the hermit should notice him, there flew down from the tree a golden parrot, which landed on his shoulder and said, "Let us go home now, Little Father, for your wife is alone. While you travel far from home, I shall tell her stories to keep her safe and well, and keep her love only for you."

With a broad smile, the Sultan fell silent, and leaned back on his cushions.

"Ahh," said Eldest Brother, echoed by the others in the room. "And did the golden parrot tell the wife stories?"

The Sultan nodded.

"And did the parrot keep the wife faithful to the merchant?"

"The merchant," replied the Sultan, "was content."

"And did you hear any of the stories told by the golden parrot?" asked Scheherazade.

"I did," beamed the Sultan, waving away all expressions of praise for his telling. "But, you, the one who is not Zuphasta and not Elder Brother. You have eaten and drunk. I have already heard the stories told by the golden parrot, but I have not heard the one you are going to tell us. It is you who must speak."

"In my father's kingdom," the young man began, "it was in ancient times the custom for the eldest son, the one who would become king, to go with his twelve closest friends out to kidnap brides for themselves. It was a custom that came from an even more ancient time when all the men of the tribe raided other tribes and the villages of the settled farmers to find and capture brides. In these days, the prince and his chosen friends go forth from the kingdom to win brides for themselves through great deeds of courage or of wit."

"Ahh," responded the Sultan, beaming.

"And . . . ahh . . . what of a king who was the father of daughters?" asked Eldest Brother, who was himself the father of five.

My great-grandmother was the one and only child of her parents, the one in whom all their love and hope resided, replied the young man. When it was time for her to marry, she, who was called Anniko, took her bow, her sword, and her horse and rode out to find a husband worthy of her hand. Riding through many kingdoms, including one that was composed entirely of warrior-women, she saw and learned many things.

After some time, she happened upon a solitary figure, somber and alone at a well on the edge of a vast and deserted plain. The person did not look up at her approach, nor at her greeting. She dismounted, gave her horse to drink, and looked at this lonely person. Head bowed, the figure did not return her glance, as it had ignored her greeting. At last, her horse rested and her own thirst slaked, she remounted and prepared to leave, much mystified by this strange one who stood there alone, silent, without mount, so far from human habitation.

As she started to ride away, a deep voice called to her. "You seem to be one unafraid. Can you help one who is cursed?"

"How can I help?" she replied.

"Perhaps no one can." With a sigh, throwing back the hood of his cloak, the solitary stranger sat down upon a rock near the well.

"Ten years ago," he began, "the time had come for me to take a wife. This I did, amidst great merrymaking. It was the union of two noble families, made in a time of great promise. There was such joy!"

Dismounting from her horse, Anniko sat where she could see the one who had declared himself cursed.

"On our wedding night, we retired to our chambers, accompanied by music and singing in the courtyard beneath our window. After a time, the household was silent. After a time, everyone slept. And when I awoke, I was alone in our marriage chamber. My bride was gone. Only her garments remained."

"She had been stolen away from your very home?" asked Anniko, horrified.

"Worse," replied the sorrowful man. "There was an odor in our bridal chamber, a dreadful smell, that of roasting flesh."

Anniko shuddered.

"The rest of the story is equally terrible," said the stranger.

"That cannot be," replied Anniko.

"After two years, I dared to marry again. Surely the disappearance of my first bride had been a mystery. Perhaps she had been carried off by a wicked Djinn. My people urged me to marry, saying that we must have an heir, and so I married again."

"And?"

"It was the same."

"The same?"

"I, too, asked myself how I could have failed to protect my bride. How could someone have entered and left that place? I know only that we slept. But I know I could never do such a thing. . . ." He sighed. "There is more to this curse . . . something . . . worse."

"How?"

"Three times my brides have been taken. Three times there has been the smell of roasted flesh in an empty room, save only that I was there. And, after such a terrible happening, the kingdom rose up against me, and I was attacked. Those who believed in me are all slain. But I cannot be slain."

"You are invincible. Ahh. I have heard of such magic," said Anniko. "Your people now believe that you have made a pact with some evil spirit, perhaps even that you *are* an evil spirit. It is only in that manner that one cannot be slain."

"True." The stranger sighed. "My people will not have me. Death refuses me."

"Were all three weddings," asked Anniko, "in the same room, in the same place?"

"No. The first was in my own palace. The second was in the palace of my father-in-law. For the third, the only one who has always been and is now faithful to me, my vizir, prepared a marriage tent on sacred ground. Changing the place did nothing to avoid the evil."

"Was there any garment, jewel, any object that was in the room every time?"

"Only my miserable cursed self," replied the sorrowful king.

Anniko stood up and walked over to where the king sat. She looked at him for a long time. Yes, evil can appear pleasing to the eye and to the ear. This somber, gentle man, whose troubles had touched his hair and beard with gray . . . no. He was innocent.

"It is only your brides who disappear," she asked, "or concubines as well?"

"Marriage alone seems forbidden to me," he replied.

"Then, if we are to lift this curse," she said, "I suppose we must be married."

Together they walked, leading Anniko's horse, back to his city, to the house of his only remaining friend, the one who was vizir. As they walked, Anniko asked a great many questions of the king. Only once did she make any reply.

When they appeared at his gate, the vizir himself opened it to them. "Ahh, my king and my friend"—he embraced the king, weeping—"the servants saw you coming from afar. And have your prayers been answered?"

"This maiden, who will be queen in her own land, which is far, far away, has consented to be my wife. Because of the great sorrows of our kingdom, we shall have only a modest ceremony, in my palace."

"Oh, my king and friend, is that wise? All the people are afraid to enter your palace. Who will protect you?"

"In this terrible thing, no one has been able to protect . . . my brides," replied the king.

"At your command," replied the vizir, bowing.

The marriage ceremony was performed. Afterward, the king and Anniko sat through the wedding dinner but touched neither food nor drink. Afterward, they were led by the vizir to the royal bedchamber, where they sat themselves down upon cushions, their swords and bows close at hand. Bowing his forehead to the floor, the vizir wished them joy and long life and many sons and daughters to follow them. They replied with thanks, and the vizir left the room, closing the doors behind him. They were alone in that vast palace.

For hours, they played at chess, told one another stories, sang songs to one another, waiting and watching for what would come. The moon rose and set. The king, who had begun to nod, got up from his place, saying, "Shall we walk awhile to help us remain awake?"

Anniko, taking up her sword in her hand, stood up to join him.

But even as the king leaned down to pick up his sword, he slumped to the floor, into sleep. Anniko, feeling herself suddenly weak, took firm hold of her sword. From a place where one carpet lay close alongside another on the marble floor, green mist rose toward her. Growing even larger and thicker, it took shape. Red eyes gleaming, its tongue blood-red, teeth brown with dried blood, brown saliva dripping, the monster rushed toward her. Swinging her sword, Anniko called out to the king but could make no sound. Ducking under the green arms that reached for her, she pricked the king's foot with her sword. With a cry, he sprang up, fully awake, took up his sword, and together they slashed and cut at the monster, meanwhile chanting prayers against this evil. The king's voice could be heard echoing in the chamber, but Anniko's made not a sound.

Hours passed, and still they struggled. Then, as each stroke with the heavy swords grew weaker, the first light of dawn filtered into the room. The monster shrank from the light, grew steadily smaller until there remained on the floor a single, bloody object, a human finger.

"What is this?" asked the king.

"Do not touch it," warned Anniko, her voice no longer stilled by the power of the monster. "The one who has made an agreement with this evil Djinn will come here for it."

Hours passed. No one came. They, exhausted, waited. The sun was high when there came a gentle tapping on the chamber door. Anniko, sword in hand, went to open it. Bowing again and again, saying again and again how blessed this kingdom was to have the curse ended, the vizir appeared, accompanied by a multitude of nobles, officials of the kingdom, citizens, and palace servants. One after another, they entered the chamber, bowing and singing praises. All the while, the king and Anniko replied courteously, never taking their eyes from the gruesome object on the floor. Thus it was that the vizir found himself, in spite of the crush of people in the room, touched by the points of two swords when he stooped to pick up the finger, the finger he had cut from his own right hand.

Poor king, how painful it was for him to learn that his trusted friend, his vizir, highest noble in the land, had so wanted to be king that he had made a most dreadful pact with an evil Djinn. The Djinn, after so long a time without a king's bride for its meal, had been prepared to eat both king *and* bride that wedding night, but had to content itself with the vizir instead—on the night that followed.

The no longer sad king made one new law that day, a law permitting himself to choose a successor from among the wisest and bravest in the kingdom and then to leave. Thus it was that the sad king became happy.

"Ah," said Eldest Brother. "And became your great-grandfather. . . . Excellent family. . . . And then, not so long ago, a great-grandson went out to seek . . ."

"Yes, yes," urged the Sultan. "Continue."

"When the time came for me to go forth to find the one who would be my bride, queen of our kingdom, I took my horse, my sword, and my friends, and set out. We found, one by one, brides for my friends, but from the edge of my father's kingdom, in every place on our journey, I heard tell of the Princess Scheherazade, who was both wise and good and as beautiful as the full moon. On and on I traveled, until I found the town in which she lived, and there I watched and listened. I heard that the princess enjoyed a life of such serenity, such order, that nothing could tempt her to change it. As I listened, I formed my plan. I would take on a disguise, make myself a guest at her palace, then disappear, leaving behind me a household no longer serene. Then, as I had learned was her habit, the Princess Scheherazade would surely go to the desert to regain her peace. There, in the desert, I would disguise myself first as the old sheikh, then as a poor slave. I would trick her into becoming my companion in an adventure. Surely I could win her where others had failed."

"Yes, yes, surely," came the chorus of replies all around the room.

"Having made my plan, I set out to learn to disguise myself. My teacher, the one who lent me the baby elephant, did teach me but did also warn me that the pretense of disguise has its dangers."

"Indeed . . . dangers . . . difficulties . . . baby elephant." The room stirred with whispered sighs of agreement.

"I heard his words but did not listen. . . . That night"—and here the young man sighed—"I tore off the disguise in which I had appeared to her as the patriarch sheikh and became a ragged dirty fellow, a beardless youth who would save her from the anger of the sheikh's servants and family. And, pretending to be such a boy, I became more foolish than any boy."

"Tell us," urged the Sultan, "that we may hear of it."

"After our escape, we did not have the adventure I had intended. My friends were to have appeared in that village. They were to have been the caravan. With them, we were to have had wonderful adventures on our journey to the mountains of everlasting snow."

"Ahh." The Sultan's eyes glistened with pleasure.

"And when the caravan of Ghouls who had taken the form of bandits appeared, I thought how well my friends had disguised themselves. I marveled at their cleverness! Only some of the horses and camels did I recognize, and some of the saddles and blankets.

"But it was strange, how no one made a sign to me. It was strange how they said the journey would be four days when we had agreed on another plan. It was strange.

"It was Scheherazade who saved us from greasing the chins of the Ghouls with whom we journeyed. It was then I saw full well how foolish my plan had been. I felt only shame. I had everywhere mentioned the story of the Reluctant Bethrothéd Pair, a story to capture the interest of the Princess. How foolish to tell it and then to live it!" He sighed, took a deep breath, and continued.

"My companions, who were to have arrived at the deserted village to be our caravan, had, meanwhile, suffered their own misfortune. They had been struck down by some mysterious illness of the place—a fever that left them lying on their saddle blankets, too weak to fight the bandits who fell upon them, stole away the horses, camels, blankets, and saddles I later recognized.

"When my friends recovered, they—brave and loyal—went in search of us. They, together with the ones who had pretended to be the 'servants' and 'family' of the 'old sheikh,' returned the mare to this place, with messages that the Princess was safe . . . messages they could only hope were true. My friends then searched the desert far and wide for us, missing us at every turn, until we appeared at the camp of the Bedouins. In my shame, I hid myself, but have come now to beg forgiveness of the princess and her family."

"Ahh," exclaimed the Sultan, Eldest Brother, Auntie Berthe, along with all the family and guests. There followed such expressions of sympathy, of forgiveness, of praise for courage, for stories well told, which led into praise for the story told by the Sultan, and to general admiration for many fine disguises in spite of the trouble they had caused.

Scheherazade sat quietly, listening to their words and to her own thoughts. How greatly the world had changed. Some things were not as they seemed. Some things were no longer as they had been. Even the Sultan had become a teller of tales. When the one who was not Zuphasta, not Elder Brother, the prince whose name she did not know, at last raised his eyes to look at her, she spoke softly.

"Your kingdom," she asked, "how near is it to the mountains whose tops are ever white with snow?"